OBSCURE BLESSINGS

Roger Lebovitz

Fomite

Burlington VT

ISBN-13: 978-1-959984-84-9
Library of Congress Control Number: 2025933546
Fomite
58 Peru Street
Burlington, VT 05401
4/16/2025

Contents

1 For crossing a river — 1

2 For flying into the air — 4

3 For train schedules — 6

4 For journeys — 8

5 For lost things — 11

6 For fallen giants — 13

7 For music in the evenings — 16

8 For unanswered questions — 19

9 For worn-away lands — 21

10 For weariness — 23

11 For imaginary birds — 26

12 For unarrived letters — 29

13 For conjured orchestras — 31

14 For fallen-down cairns   34

15 For the childless   36

16 For fires on highways   39

17 For unvisited graves   42

18 For the high patches of snow   44

19 For the recounting of disasters   47

20 For unread dreams   49

21 For songs that stop the sea   51

22 For the ships offshore   53

23 For meaningless coincidences   56

24 For sleeping readers   58

25 For walking   61

26 For the far-off whistle   63

27 For ponds   65

28 For snakes falling out of the sky 67

29 For comets and forests 70

30 For silent swarming stars 72

31 For hauling up buckets 75

32 For the unexpected 78

33 For being forgotten 80

34 For messages on the air 83

35 For chanterelle pools 86

36 For the need for blessings 88

Appendix/Notes 92

About the Author 97

1

For crossing a river

I've always wanted to see that river, the river the
army crossed and the river where the crossing
soldiers cursed, or at least the ones that fell
off their horses and started to drown, they
cursed. What was the name of the river? There
are several options here, depending on which
language we use, depending on a number of
things such as which set of borders we recognize
or even the name of the century we find ourselves
in. The standards of sunset unfurled above us,
but that is an inexact translation. I am sorry that
I can't quote the translated phrase with any kind

of accuracy. Accuracy helps, although inaccuracy
also helps, if inaccuracy is what is needed, if
accuracy is in short supply and a substitute is
required. Some days all I can recall is a landscape
of inaccuracy. Please believe me when I say the
start of this story of the river crossing made
a significant impression on me, even if at the
end the protagonist needed to sleep next to
the murdered father so as to bring the edifice
crashing down upon its final punctuation mark.
Are we dreaming? I did make plans to gather
by that river, that beautiful river, getting there
by plane and by train and even by boat should
that have proven necessary, if that was required.
Or on foot, because they say the countryside
is lovely to walk across and you can imagine
the buckwheat fields in the distance, and then
dream about the walls of ancient monasteries. I
did make plans to translate the story, or at least
translate the first line, or at least translate the
curses of the soldiers who drowned, the ones
who slipped off their horses into the current

of the river whose name we may never recall.
But events intervened and the excursion was
postponed. The translation never happened.
We'll have to get the news another way, the news
of how the town was taken at dawn. Of course
later Tukhachevsky's army was thrown back
before reaching the capital and human events
shifted like the inaccurate tides they resemble.
Yet one day soon we'll travel down that road
built out of the bones of peasants. Please believe
me when I tell you this: A highway made of
bones, what might they think of next? The tsar
built this road, or so they say, he and his armies
crossed a river too, and likely saw the same
sunset banners, saw the same orange sun roll its
way across the ancestor of this evening's sky.

2

For flying into the air

But then we talked about Hannah and
mentioned how she prayed drunk, totally stoned
in fact. Although this wasn't the case at all, it
got written down wrong and no one thought
to correct the historical record for many years.
Next, this in turn reminded someone of an
argument over whether and how prayer might
be joyful, which reminded someone else about
how a long lost sage thought prayer must have
its portion of sorrow. This one sage showed up
at a wedding once a long time ago and began
to sing a thousand verses of the blues, and after

singing a thousand verses of the blues everyone
wanted to know, great, but what is the chorus
can we hear the chorus please? So the sage sang
about a hundred choruses and even flew a bit in
the air like the characters in those paintings by
Chagall we saw once in Montreal. But then we
talked about the fancy glass the blues-singing
sage smashed at this same wedding, although by
that time of course men on horses rode up and
slaughtered the wedding party in both Hebrew
and Aramaic and also Polish, Ukrainian and
German, if only because the universal language
had not been devised at that point in time.
Afterwards, the apple tree growing in the same
spot as the wedding survived for centuries,
even though apple trees like women and men
are allowed only three score and ten. And each
spring the apple tree filled itself with fragrant
blossoms but no apples fell the following fall. I
wonder if Hannah ever prayed beside or beneath
an apple tree. Sometimes I think she did, but
then other times I think probably not.

3

For train schedules

I cannot tell you how things might have been.
I cannot tell you his mind, or the state of his
mind. I do know that we went down to the
railroad tracks to watch the evening train headed
north to Harrisburg. This train no longer runs,
which is important only in the way important
things can be when they go about the world
disguised as inconsequential things hidden
among discarded lists. The tracks are still there,
I think, but I have not been back in some time
to confirm this and as of now have no plans to
ever return. I do remember waiting for the train

to pass, waiting for what seemed to a child to
be an indeterminable interval of unrehearsed
stillness, a time to observe the rails and the
woods opposite and recite in no organized
fashion what odd species of thoughts happened
by. I am always devising some new taxonomy of
thoughts, some hierarchy of observations that
never makes any sense, that always crumbles
after time enough and the considerations that
no one could anticipate. This habit, as far as I
can tell, dates from these excursions. In any case
the train eventually cranked by, we waved to the
engineer and waved to the passengers, some of
whom waved back. I suppose he took that train
to school, back and forth, many years before.
That was another life. And then that very train
was gone, vanished around the bend, and we sat
quite forlorn on the shore of the empty space
that remained.

4

For journeys

Here is another story I once heard: G-d said to Abraham, kill me a son (note a son, not the son or your son, which of course implies both that Abraham had more than one son and perhaps had a choice about which son to kill). Abraham, in any case, wanted no son killed and so fled with his son from G-d into the wilderness. They wandered there for quite some time, moving from watering hole to watering hole and relying on the roaming shepherds and their flocks for sustenance, in accordance with the principle of hospitality to strangers which at the time received universal observance. Perhaps the shepherds thought Abraham was a messenger from an unknown deity or from some other supernatural figure, or if neither of those then a tax collector in disguise from some far-off empire, in other words, someone to be humored at all costs. It is hard to tell what went through the minds of these men as they offered the pair mutton and milk. At last, they came to a shoreline where a man supervised the building of an enormous boat that he claimed needed to carry as many animals as he could possibly find. That guy's crazy, the townspeople said, but nevertheless Abraham asked if he and his son might join the voyage, adding that he could keep the ship's log as well as his own personal account of what was sure to be an adventure. The crazy man agreed to these terms but insisted on a written agreement, because everyone needs a contract inked and signed in order to minimize present uncertainty and posthumous confusion. (Little did Abraham know that in the ship's hold was a rather strange cargo - not animals but two of every book ever written). So they set sail and soon left sight of land. And they stayed out of sight of the land for forty days and forty nights, and no matter how hard they tried to find the land they could not find it. But at last the water drained out and the boat came to rest on the side of a mountain. Abraham and his son disembarked, but soon thereafter God, clearly displeased that his instructions had been ignored, slew them both. There is no telling how Abraham's other sons reacted to this news, whether they felt relief at having survived, whether they ever looked in any of the books that were saved, the ones that went forth and multiplied from that day forward.

5

For lost things

If you try talking about it, it all falls apart. We
still have my grandmother's silverware, the
ones with her initials, her maiden name and
married name and given name. Why did these
pieces disappear for so long? They were put
in a cardboard box hidden in a closet in the
basement, an anonymous box that escaped
attention for years, but I found it by accident
while searching, of course, for something else.
A gift on her wedding day, a few years after her
sister died in the epidemic and she embarked on
an adult life free from certain fears but not free

from the invisible fears that floated just above
the houses in the summer afternoons, as if the
details of what was invisible could somehow
be understood as an equation simplified to its
salient elements. I drag the silverware out once
or twice a year, Thanksgiving or Passover, not
entirely resisting the temptation of boring the
guests with the story of how she was rummaging
through boxes in the unfinished attic on Bateman
Ave and fell through a weak spot in the floor into
the room below, and how tragedy was averted
only because of a bed located directly below. I
realize now this is the only story I have of her,
and that repetition has simplified the telling of it.
I have a photograph where she is standing at the
bow of a boat crossing Lake Champlain, looking
at something passing by on the shore, or just
looking at the water with its myriad reflections of
the sky. Who knows? The cardboard box that hid
the silverware is still in my possession, although
it now suffers from the wear and tear native to all
things once hidden.

6

For fallen giants

Here is another story I once heard: They blinded Samson just like old Gloucester and so he had to sniff his way all over the land of the Philistines, and any citizen of that land had the right to take a lock of his hair, which they did and many of these ended up as keepsakes and handed down as family heirlooms. Eventually, the authorities put Samson in a cage in the palace where they charged the locals a dollar or two to stand around and just watch the fallen giant, the slayer of so many of their troops, (what a

bargain said everyone waiting in line) just to
observe the bloody orbs, to gawk at the vile
jellies now caked and dried on his cheek. After
weeks and months sight returned to Samson,
his eyes and sight grew back, like the sprouts
that crown a tree stump. But he did not see
the bright colors that previously populated
his visions, only dim shapes, broad outlines,
nothing of their interiors defined. He had
to guess, to estimate, to resign himself to
inhabiting this new netherworld. But this was
sufficient. The story from this point on does
not bear repeating because you have doubtless
heard it many times before. Afterwards, the
scavengers picked through the destroyed
palace, they gathered up the broken pieces
of the architecture in their sacks, they slung
the sacks over their shoulders and vanished
into the wilderness, headed towards the lands
beyond where they exchanged these sacks of
ruins for other means of sustenance. These
broken pieces turn up every now and then in

disparate places, on pawn shop shelves, in the indexes of old books, half-buried beneath the winter grasses of empty lots.

7

For music in the evenings

Sparrows are intelligent and pretty birds said to
recite never-ending monologues to themselves
as they fly. Some claim to hear the word of G-d
in these monologues, and this inspires them
to attempt to put out the sparrow's eyes. Yet
despite this on certain summer evenings, one
or two sparrows comprise the audience for the
violinists who play at the base of the monument
to the Civil War dead, where General Sheridan
gave a speech and a misfired salute blew off
a young man's arm, although fortunately the
young man was later granted a pension by the

state legislature. I know a violinist who goes
to the monument almost every evening when
the weather is warm and dry, she plays bits and
pieces from concertos and also folk songs that
may have been collected years ago by ethnologists
who were also serious composers and then
emigrated due to the political situation. She
keeps her case open and every so often a sparrow
flits to the edge of the open case, the bird turns
its little head this way and that as if listening
to the music, when of course the bird is really
looking this way and that into the case with its
worn velvet interior thinking maybe there is a
crumb or two in there for it to eat. The violinist
sometimes leaves a crumb or two on purpose
because she believes all sentient beings need to
eat, and after all music is better enjoyed on a full
stomach. But the sparrow did listen to the songs,
and also it seemed it had favorite songs as well.
If you were a musician you could do worse than
have an audience of sparrows or even a single
sparrow, turning its head this way and that,

fluffing its wings, and at the end of a song giving out an appreciative little cheep, then flitting away to recite another installment of its never-ending monologue.

8

For unanswered questions

Could you answer the question in any other
way? But here was the secret. The question had
no answer. So they kept asking more questions,
and each subsequent question begat another
generation of questions and on and on and on.
And while some questions survived only their
allotted three score and ten, others kept being
asked for hundreds of years, and longer. Yet at
times it seemed they were on the verge of an
answer, while at other times the answer seemed
so far away that they decided the better course of
action would be to go back over all the questions

trying to find the original question, stepping
back through thousands of questions, reasoning
ultimately that if the answers eluded them
they might as well have the first question on
hand, and if they found this first question they
might start over with the answering. Only this
time finding the correct response from the very
beginning. This is what they thought. But this
search proved far more difficult than anticipated.
It turned out there was no simple way back to
the first question, the path was threaded and
frayed as if a great river's delta tied itself into
knots. One esteemed scholar would say to turn
here, while another esteemed scholar would insist
on turning there, and the entire affair became
hopelessly muddled. Finally someone stumbled
on the secret - none of the questions had any
answers. But no one could believe this, because
the secret to them seemed just like any other
question. Because not having an answer was just
another way of asking a question.

9

For worn-away lands

The swifts return each May after flying thousands of miles from another continent. I have never been quite sure where they winter or how they travel the long distances from their wintering ground to their summer homes. They nest inside chimneys, and on warm evenings you can hear how they are calling to one another high up in the middle of the air, and watch their little bodies flit up and down in great near-invisible motions. The brick chimneys in which they put their nests are made out of clay found on the floor of the old sea that vanished thousand years ago. This clay represents the smallest particle of the lands worn away by the rivers that carried their burdens to this old sea. So that each nest is built inside a tower risen, in fact, from the bottom of the ocean. The chimney bricks are fired in a process as old, perhaps, as the Tower of Babel. It is said that once the Tower had been destroyed, the remnant still standing hosted a colony of swift nests for many years afterwards. If you look carefully at Brueghel's painting of the Tower you might imagine a few spots in the sky that could be swifts, and the swift's call may well retain some of the sound of the universal language spoken before the Tower's destruction. But this is all speculation. Yet I firmly believe nothing can be truly desolate if there are swifts. When they return in the spring and I look up in the sky to see them, it seems as if they never left. As if there were no such thing as a vacant sky.

10

For weariness

Where had he been, Lord Randall? He was
someone's handsome young man, that much is
clear. In other words he came in from the woods
but something had happened in those woods.
Think about the things that can happen in
the woods, people getting lost, people meeting
strangers, small planes crashing far from any
road and then fog grounds the search flights for
days and the survivors succumb to the elements.
Sometimes in the woods there is a puddle that
magically becomes a lake or vice versa, although
at other times the puddle dries up into a patch

of sand. Is this a puddle or a lake, you have to decide, and as always there are consequences if you choose wrong. There is no telling if Lord Randall saw any of this, if he survived a plane clash or walked across a barren sand patch or met a fair young maiden that promised him to wed but gave him poisoned eels instead, eels fried in a pan, perhaps, fried on a campfire that Lord Randall himself may have kindled. The fair maiden was never given a song, or if she was given a song no collectors have yet hauled that song up in their nets. And yet their collections are the only instruments we have, the only instruments to determine what trees were in the woods, were they beech, were they oak, were they maple, had the underbrush been cleared by fire or the overbrowsing of forest beasts. The collections are the only instruments we have to measure what the weather was like when Lord Randall came in from the woods. It must have have been a summer's day. That should be obvious from centuries of recitation and commentary. The sun shone for long hours and the shadows at noon were short and in the late evening, the twilight lingered against the trunks of the maple, oak, and beech. Summer twilight is a welcome guest. It was then that Lord Randall, that handsome young man, stumbles in from the wood. Because that's where he had been. He is weary, he would gladly lie down, and mother makes his bed soon.

11

For imaginary birds

There was no path along the river. So they navigated around the imaginary lakes and fished trout from the waters with rods found hanging inside a moose's skeleton. In the empty cabins they read novels by Eugene Sue, deeming the remainder trash, and speculated on how to make the ashy soul say tomatoes or beans on the pages of short growing seasons. When at last they reached the higher ground, our hero set off on a bearing towards recklessly heaped and honest New England granite of the mile-high sort. Jackson measured the altitude here

in 1837. But then a kind of insanity struck
him, as if he thought he would never escape the
cloud that refused to quit the summit, as if the
jumble of rocks might remain the last landscape
he would ever see. He fell and skinned his shin
and wondered for a moment at the sight of this
unimportant blood, and in the next instant it
was as if the wind blew a flock of sparrows out
of the rocks, it was as if the wind made the rocks
into the sparrows themselves, and twisted the
flock of them this way and that. These were
imaginary birds, although later he did see and
hear real ones. He knew their calls, he sang to
them, and they told him what awaited upstream
on the Penobscot, if he ever made it that far. If
at times it seemed as if the cloud would lift, in
the end it never did, even though in his mind
he peopled the future of the countryside with
cloud factories as far as the eye could see. In the
end, he retreated back to his companions who
had spent the morning dining on blueberries
and cranberries, then paddled back to Bangor by

shooting the rapids in the expert batteaus. On
the last leg of the journey on the steamer back to
Boston, he had a dream that put him at the top
of the tallest pine tree where he had climbed to
get a view of the landscape and become unlost,
because that was how it was done back then in
forests stretching all the way to Canada. But
before he could get his bearings the swaying of
the treetop in the wind made him faint and he
fell down from one branch to the other. But each
branch transferred the essayist downward from
one to another with love and care, the trees knew
that here was a man who loved their needles and
leaves, their barks and roots, and this descent,
once accomplished, made for a consolation prize
for not making the summit, until at the end he
stood on the firmer and level ground that poses
sometimes as the exit from journeys and dreams.

12

For unarrived letters

When his father died they held a funeral, but
before the funeral itself they brought the coffin
into a room and they said do you want us to
open the coffin so you can have one last look.
And some said yes we want one last look but
others insisted no, under no circumstances do
we want one last look. And the ones who wanted
one last look asked those who refused to look
why they refused to look and the ones who
refused said: we will not tell you. But maybe, they
added later, but maybe we will send you a letter
in a few years that explains why we refused to

look. So the ones who looked waited a long time for the letter from the ones who refused to look to finally come, they waited each day to see if that letter might be in the mailbox but it never was. But could you imagine in the story about the wife of Lot and about Lot himself, if the wife of Lot had said, no, I refuse to look, I refuse to turn around and look, and Lot had said, but you have to look, you have to turn around and look and be turned into salt because that is the way this story must unfold and ultimately end. Could you imagine this, for example. So they waited for the letter to arrive, the letter the people who did not look promised to send, and one day it did arrive but in the envelope there was no letter. They opened the envelope expecting a letter of explanation because a long awaited explanation is a powerful thing, it has qualities not fully understood by the instruments we possess that purport to measure all creation. But when they opened the envelope there was no letter. There was just a pinch of salt.

13

For conjured orchestras

"Daily rainstorms, unbearable heat, astonishing
costumes, disorder on the street." Yet he
continued to haul his heavy Edison cylinders in
a one-wheeled cart from one village to another,
where on a daily basis peasants lined up to sing
into the wide horn as the needle etched the song
into the wax. Think of these transformations
for a moment here: from song to wax to the
ear of Bartok, who transcribed the sung notes
to written ones caught in the net of five-lined
staves. So the song had a life cycle of its own, it
began in a woman's heart and ended on a page,

it began in a woman's heart two hundred years
before. But at times something went wrong
and too many notes stuck to the staves and he
ended up with an impenetrable underbrush of
sounds, while at other times there were too few
notes and it looked like a field where the corn
came up too weakly because of drought and he
could barely salvage the few notes that made
up the scale which nonetheless was unlike any
scale ever heard before. Did the singers know
this fate awaited their songs? Later accounts
claimed Bartok could conjure the tunes out of
air and needed only to gesture with his hand
this way and that for the melodies to sound
aloud -- although no one could be seen singing
them. Or that wasn't it exactly, he conjured
whole orchestras out of passers-by, making
anonymous commuters into virtuosos. For this
the Regent wanted to put out his eyes and cut
off his ears, but the composer escaped on a boat,
although he died later in an apartment building
in Manhattan. In the end they determined the

wax cylinders were just for show. They were just a decoy, something to keep the blessed from hearing the melodies they had no right to hear.

14

For fallen-down cairns

The manuscripts tell of how Simon flew and
was destroyed. The manuscripts also tell of
how Simon was buried alive and was destroyed.
There are eyewitness accounts, or at least
the manuscripts claim there were eyewitness
accounts, they say Peter and his disciples
witnessed these events, and also ordinary
townsfolk watched as Simon ascended to a
speck of a point high up in the sky, and they also
watched as the coffin with Simon inside was
lowered into the hole the townspeople dug deep
into the sand. In any case, they dug the coffin up

and found Simon still alive and unperturbed,
and the adherents of the messiah cult were
immediately drummed out of the town. Yet in
another account, the coffin contained only a mass
of putrid flesh, and Peter and his compatriots
would have grinned in triumph if they could
have stood the stench. Either ending confirms
something we have always suspected. And
wasn't there an account of Simon flying above
the buildings in Rome with the Emperor as
witness, with the Emperor staring crane-necked
slack-jawed as Simon flew freely through the
naked air? This failed too, the same as that boy
who came too near the sun and found not only
could he not fly, but he also could not swim. Yet
each of these accounts and similar ones add their
little stone to the edifice, stone upon stone upon
stone so that at last there is a cairn on a hilltop
wordlessly commemorating all events. People
passing by touch these stones, they reach out and
the very touch of flesh on stone calms them. So
that after many years they are worn smooth.

15

For the childless

If you gather 'round me people, a story I will
tell. And they paid attention young and old,
and soon everyone in their heads could picture
Pretty Boy Floyd who had come to beg a meal
at the side door of the dusty farmhouse, and
they could see how the farmer and his wife let
him in, even though they may have been a little
suspicious of this stranger, because those were
the days of suspicions and strangers, and dust
clouds blowing high into the air. Imagine this
as an old newsreel and the people hurk and jerk
in accordance with the strict rules of frames-

36

per-second of that historical era. Of course, the couple were barren, the song didn't mention this, but anyone listening knew this already, that's just how it was back in those days. So they fed Pretty Boy Floyd and he ate what they ate - soup with a little chicken maybe or likely without, beans sweetened with molasses, a loaf of bread the farmer sliced using a knife with a worn rosewood handle (the natural history of this knife being recounted in another well-known song). And when the meal was done and the table cleared, that was when Pretty Boy Floyd slipped the thousand dollar bill under the napkin, he did this with an unrehearsed virtuosic gesture, a graceful movement that should have been enshrined in ballet or honored in pantomime, the thousand dollar bill that showed the face of Wilson upon his triumphant return from Versailles, Wilson before a stroke and the Senate laid him low. The silent thousand dollar lay there silently, the napkin covered it like the uncut grass covers a grave. And it was still there, waiting patiently

underneath the napkin a full half an hour after
Pretty Boy said thank you and good bye, and
after shaking hands with each of them, vanished
into the hot quiet of the afternoon. And was the
couple blessed with a child? The song never said.

16

For fires on highways

Think about the imaginary fires on the
interstates and how no one has written their
history. Think about all those nights you drove
along those empty highways themselves. There
was the presence of a river sensed on the right-
hand side even if no one sees the river itself.
There was the shadow of a mountain on the
left-hand side that held the place where the
mountain itself no doubt presided in daylight.
Because there are daylight mountains and there
are mountains at night and there are rivers at
night and rivers in broad daylight. This was

somewhere between Ascutney and Montpelier.
For a long time you saw nothing and the
darkness begat mere darkness until all of a
sudden there it was, like a house on fire. And it
was a house on fire, in the middle of the highway.
But what sort of house with what sort of rooms
and walls and floors and ceilings? Yet not a
house at all as you drove through it, you drove
into and out of the bright fire of the imaginary
and nearly hallucinatory flames that could have
been an old farmhouse from so many years ago.
You made it through and then looking back
through the mirror you saw no light, you saw
no flames but only the same darkness. It might
have been Romaine Tenney's house or the house
of someone else who burned down their house
just before the new systems of transportation
overcame them. Someday you'll write this
history you tell yourself, this history of imaginary
fires on the interstates and also on other roads,
although at the end of the book there'll be no
light but only the same darkness. When Troy fell,

they lit fires on watchtowers and mountain tops
to spread the news of the Achaean's triumph.
Think then of how many years men spent
watching, looking into the dark, waiting for a
signal.

17

For unvisited graves

At this point, come to a full stop and take a
breath. There once was a writer, you'll remember,
who lost his daughter in Geneva, perhaps
because he couldn't pay for a decent doctor
and so diphtheria carried the poor thing off.
This was because he needed to pay the debts
his dead brother incurred and also support his
stepchildren, ungrateful. He visited the child's
grave every day but then they had to leave
Geneva because he couldn't stand the Swiss.
Nevertheless he still kept sending bits of his
novel back to the capitol, where piece by piece

the editors of magazines reassembled it like
some bomb designed to blow up a government
official or a debating society, or like a lurching
automaton meant to bring peace to all mankind
or tear it to pieces. The writer and his wife went
on to Prague but couldn't find an apartment
to rent, then returned to Germany. But keep
in mind that the order in which details are
recounted is less important than it seems. He
returned to his child's graveside only once, years
later, and if he ever returned again, this has never
been recorded. Perhaps the account of this final
return has been lost, like so many other things.
What could it possibly mean? In any case, for a
long time I looked for a picture of this little girl's
grave, but never found it.

18

For the high patches of snow

Darby Field founded a kingdom of snow patches.
He claimed melting snow patches up on the
high terrain in what is now considered to be
New Hampshire, but claimed also the rivers
and streams loaded with meltwater surging
down the mountains towards the sea which at
that point in time went largely unmapped. The
snow fields atop the mountains were his domain,
but they shrank each day as the spring months
tilted themselves toward summer and the vast
snowfields became mere patches. He planted
a flag, his own personal flag and not the flag of

any nation or king, on these patches and claimed
each one of them for a kind of greater glory
only he could define, only he could articulate.
He explained this glory to the cliffs and talus
on the mountain, and they all agreed with him.
He sat at the base of temporary waterfalls and
transcribed their wisdom. As the patches shrank
his flags had nothing to support them and fell
down, he left dozens of flags struck down on
the top of the mountain, and it seemed as if an
invisible army had surrendered for unknown
reasons. Until at last he confined himself to a
single patch of snow, the final one left, but like
Antaeus touching the earth touching snow was
how he derived his power. Towards the end
of his life, he would go insane and be confined
to a small cottage on the sea coast. History
remembers him as the first white man to climb
Mount Washington, and does not remember
his kingdom at all. What was this kingdom he
founded and why did he stake his claim to these
diminished things? If you drive south in May

from Gorham you can still see these patches up on the high terrain, where they have remained unclaimed for centuries.

19

For the recounting of disasters

If Pippin had actually survived the wreck, had
floated to the surface, and been picked up by
the Rachel, we might imagine with only a little
difficulty a future for him as a performer with
a traveling circus. So come in under a small
tent to watch Pip the Whaling Boy regale the
paying customers with tales of how mountains of
leviathans were dispatched into blubber and oil,
how the iron harpoons sizzled through the air,
how the ship plunged down canyons of waves,
and how Captain Ahab and the Pequod met
their doom at the hands of Moby Dick. Because

that's how it is, we want the survivors of the
disaster to recount it over and over, thinking only
of our own pleasure. Perched up on a stool on a
temporary stage, keeping the same lookout night
after night, Pip saws the air with his hands and
sometimes even kicks his feet as if swimming to
stay afloat in the immensity of his stories. What
did they think watching this out-of-breath little
boy run through an evening full of ever-growing
exaggerations? Night after night enough of them
crowded into his tent, throwing their coins into
the box, clink-clank, each coin a cousin to a link
in a chain, coins enough to pay for his room and
board, even in desolate railroad siding towns,
even in places now erased from maps (take out
a map and try to look at them if you disbelieve
this). And after the last customer departed and
they struck the tent, Samson the Giant Tall Man
held Pip's hand as they walked across the dusty
field to their sleeping quarters. Did he dream of
Connecticut or of Alabama?

20

For unread dreams

Old men with hollow chests play shuffleboard
at the retirement home. The place is ringed
with chain link fence, barbed wire, watchtowers.
Because that's the way we do things nowadays,
you can't be too careful and it's safety now,
safety tomorrow, and safety forever. After
shuffleboard and the other games, they'll wheel
the old men back to the dining hall for the usual
supper of pureed fruits and vegetables and
prescription strength beer, after which they'll be
singing and clapping exercises, healthy minds
in healthy bodies of course, it's almost a credo

and could well be emblazoned on the gates of
the institution itself. Then it's off to bed, where
the staff hook the old men up to the dream
recording machines, which spit out a nightly
harvest of each man's dreams. Each night the
pile of unread dreams grows higher and higher,
a deplorable situation that is only now coming
to the attention of a wider public. Fortunately,
the old men at the retirement home are still kept
unaware of this situation. Who wants worry at
the end of a long and tiresome lifetime?

21

For songs that stop the sea

And what about Chet Baker who held the sea storm back by playing his horn? He stood on the beach in the teeth of of the gale and played those notes that only he knew, the secret notes he found just by wandering up and down the scales and wasn't it a surprise that nobody had found these scales before Chet Baker found them. He stood on the beach and the wind whipped the sea spume all around him, these same waters that once caressed the sides of whales and other unknown creatures, and he played and played and played and eventually the storm abated and

the sea settled down. But the effort of playing
back the sea exhausted him, and he was forced
to retire to cold water flats where he spent most
of his time looking out the window, putting his
trumpet to his lips every now and then but then
setting it down unplayed, although he did play
a few gigs every so often. In the end, the people
living in the town he saved had forgotten him,
they went about their daily lives and barely
remembered the storm and remembered not at
all the trumpet player who held it back. Chet
Baker recorded a few more albums, some of them
critically acclaimed, before falling to his death
from the second story balcony of a hotel in the
Netherlands while trying to feed crumbs to the
pigeons.

22

For the ships offshore

David Lyle wrote letters to poets and other well-known people, lengthy digressions on issues of the day and his own philosophic interpretations of the same. You have to admire this approach, sending out missives with no expectation of reply, practicing a kind of charity with no conception of charity, although at times a few poets did include parts of the letters in some of their poems. The art of letter writing is now nearly dead and we have no choice but to romanticize it. Lyle worked in aircraft and radio factories before retiring to his epistolary existence, and I

wonder if he helped put together those vacuum
tubes that powered radios back in those days.
I once worked for a union that began in the
radio machine shops, they went out on strike for
better hours, wages and working conditions in
places like Schenectady and Paterson, although
sometimes it seems they should have seized
the vacuum tubes themselves and taken to the
airwaves with their demands and with the good
news of the new economy that we all know, alas,
never happened. This reminds me of those pirate
radio stations that operate on ships offshore,
beyond any jurisdiction, and broadcast their
important messages free of any regulation or
oversight. So we might imagine David Lyle
the letter-writer and vacuum tube assembler
swimming out to one of these rusty vessels
anchored past the three mile limit, doing the old
Australian crawl through choppy waters, and by
the time he reaches the ship he is exhausted and
drenched to the bone and has barely the strength
to climb aboard, make his way below deck to the

radio room and flick the transmitter on (click,
sudden light and swivel of dials and meters) and
begin the recitation of his letters on the air.

23

For meaningless coincidences

My sole possession, as it turns out, is an ever-growing inventory of meaningless and often mistaken coincidences. For a long while, I thought that Lou Gehrig and Bruno Shulz died on the same day. This turned out not to be the case. They died a year and a half apart, and in circumstances quite dissimilar. Gehrig died in a hospital where his body deserted him while Shulz was gunned down in the street of a former Hapsburg city. Gehrig hit baseballs over fences, while Shulz wrote stories where autumn and clothing shops played prominent roles, and also taught at the local gymnasium. It is difficult to connect these items and I have to admit that after long attempts I came nowhere near success. I do know that Schulz translated Kafka into Polish, while Gehrig (I suppose) never read Kafka, despite the German he grew up with. Yet Gehrig went to the opera and cried because he understood more of life than all the other first basemen combined. And the next day he strode to the plate and hit a home run and even later stepped shyly up to a microphone and declared himself the luckiest man alive. All the while Schulz taught high school art, made drawings and wrote stories, and kept writing a novel about how the world might be saved (a novel since lost, although many have tried and failed to recover it). No part of this was able to save him in the end, just as Gehrig's tears at the opera house did not save him. What are we to make from all of this? If both had survived, what then?

24

For sleeping readers

"When I was sleepy I used to go to bed, yet as I lay there I still read something or other."

(Nathaniel Wanley, The Wonders of the Little World).

So after you fall asleep and yet continue reading there is a metamorphosis that occurs within the book at hand. It slips the bounds of the printed pages, and at times substantially rewrites itself. While you are asleep the book becomes a new book, one never seen before in the waking world. I once had a colleague at school who fell asleep reading Lear and imagined a new play where

the King and the Fool exchanged places. So that
after being awakened you may remember reading
the book but can subsequently never find the
chapters or sentences you read while asleep, even
though you remember reading them, sometimes
exactly. At times the sleeping reader will night
walk with a book in hand and read aloud, but
what they are reading aloud is not the book
they are holding in their hands but a book their
sleeping minds create. These people should not
be disturbed, however clumsy their walking may
appear; at times the shock of being awakened is
such that they lose the ability to read altogether
and must be taught everything they once knew
all over again in a years-long endeavor. According
to some what is read aloud by these walkers is
nothing less than prescient observations about
details of the future. Yet there are accounts of
those so taken with what they read while asleep
that they train themselves to sleep for many
days at a time, forgoing all of their obligations
and responsibilities in the process. There are

more of these people in the world than you
might suppose, and in some ways they resemble
the thirty-six just persons on whom continued
existence depends.

25

For walking

Robert Walser wrote stories in microscopic script
and also took a balloon ride in 1908 across the
countryside from Bittfeld to the Baltic Sea. He
wrote about that as well. Clumsiness prevented
him from tying a knot for a proper noose in the
attic apartments he rented cheaply, and perhaps
because of this he spent most of the rest of his
life in insane asylums, first in Waldau and then
in Herisau. Yet they allowed him out for walks,
sometimes alone, sometimes accompanied by
a friend who recorded his impressions of these
excursions. He walked quite far at times and

frequently enjoyed wine and meals, or just a loaf of bread, at train station restaurants and in the towns he passed through on foot, where he was not shy about expressing his opinions. No one could say precisely why he was confined to these institutions, yet it made a certain sense to him as by his own account he was there to be mad. Perhaps it had to do with the failures in faraway places and in life he could not shake off. He never achieved any sort of success while alive, and given what we know about this, there may have been a kind of logic at work when one morning he was found collapsed in the snow, his body sprawled out and his hat rolled off a little ways as if it were a separate entity with an existence purely of its own devising. Shortly afterward, this scene, for reasons no one understands even today, became the subject of a dutifully popular photograph reprinted in a number of prestigious journals and magazines.

26

For the far-off whistle

We now find our hero just after his latest official
discharge from the sanitarium, waiting at the
local train station for the express back to the city.
He holds a ticket in his hand, which proves to
all the world that he has been cured. But what is
unknown to him at that moment is how out of
date his timetable is, and how the express train
does not run on certain days, and how today is
one of those days. Certainty, in fact, drains out of
the day, it drains out of the sky and the distant
hills. After watching a number of local and
freight trains crank by he notices how quickly

evening starts in those mountain towns, and that he is not one mile closer to home. He listens for the whistle of his train, imagines it, harmonizes with what he imagines. It almost sounds like a song he once heard someone sing but now can scarcely remember. But there is no train. It is hopeless he says to himself, somewhat awkwardly because his stay at the sanitarium was mostly to treat hopelessness, and he lies down on a wooden bench and falls into a heavy and dreamless sleep despite the coolness of the evening. After a while stationmaster comes out and puts a blanket over the sleeping form. Because why not? This is the way the world ought to work, if only we took a moment to understand it.

27

For ponds

Almost independence day and we went to the
unknown pond and at night we hear the toads
trilling, a sound I have always loved, although
surprised to hear them that late in the season
even up at three thousand feet above sea level,
almost two months later than at our local
abandoned red sandrock quarry. I suppose it's
been a strange year, snow in May then a heat
wave a week later, and since then dreams about
runoff each night, usually towards morning,
cascades rushing down hillsides draining the
mountain of its snow fields. The toads' trilling

calls are like a dial tone harmonized, I dislike
this prosaic analogy but can think of no other.
Yet there may well be a little poetry in it. I listen
to the trill and then hear it an octave higher, and
next perhaps a fifth lower, it goes on all night,
a reply to the unheard hum of the universe.
Imagine you made a call from one of those old
glass phone booths on a forgotten street corner,
as ridiculous as that seems, and then were
disconnected, click thunk, you'd then hear the
dial tone that could well be toad song. In that
case you'd try listening for as long as you could,
waiting maybe for someone to pick up after all,
before hanging up.

28

For snakes falling out of the sky

I've always wanted to tell a story, don't you see, about how the Split Rock lightkeeper went out for an afternoon row on the lake and suddenly found a rattle snake (Crotalus horridus) falling into his boat from a perch atop the palisade cliffs. The snake sunning itself on the rocks atop the cliffs found itself falling through the unexpected air of the clear morning. Landing with a thunk, dazed but not dead, at the bottom of the boat. Why not have snakes fall out of the sky? This happens more often than you'd think likely. So here we might see another situation where time

is of the essence and the moment ripe for action.
Does the lightkeeper take an oar and fling the
snake out of the boat with immediate grace (the
snake's length sailing through air forms the shape
of a letter from an unknown alphabet), or does
the cornered snake strike an arm or a leg, its bite
condemning the man to a slow floating death on
the calm waters? (Although the bite from these
snakes can be fatal this is not assured, and again
we must use our imaginations). An alternate
scenario might find the boat tipped over by
understandably sudden movements on the part
of both parties, and so we see both the snake and
the man swimming for shore (snakes are natural
swimmers, men less so). They swim in the same
direction and reach land about the same time,
after which their fates, for several moments so
tightly intertwined, diverge. They never meet
again. The lightkeeper then had a long walk
back over the mountain and up along the road,
reaching the light just as the twilight commenced
its process of self-extinguishment and the time of

watching for ships began. The snake lives on for
another twenty years, spending the winters in the
subterranean rocks among hundreds of its kind,
and others.

29

For comets and forests

The soldiers hunted for the prisoner. How she
escaped no one knew. A comet appeared in the
sky and we looked for it. At that time we lived
in old wooden houses built from Laurentide
forests divided into parts and floated down rivers
and lakes in previous centuries. The sawdust
from these lumberyards that made the forests
into rafters and joists is now solid earth. From
the parapet above the lumberyards, Whitman's
brother-in-law painted landscapes, and claimed
the sunsets were the second best on the planet.
The prisoner was mad, they claimed, she slipped

in and out of the kitchen gardens at night and hid in the corners of chicken coops with the sleeping hens. What will happen when they find her? The soldiers billeted in the synagogues lost their place in the prayer book, which often occurs in the midst of military campaigns. If they could find the prisoner by praying, that might occur, because the alternative would be to keep a diary and hope she appeared in a future entry. Everything must have its official record. One soldier did keep a diary, published years later when the perspective of time gives insight on the meanings of things. At last we saw the comet in the clear early morning sky, fleeing the sun. We will likely never see it again.

30

For silent swarming stars

After they murdered the king, the night
watchman had to seek employment elsewhere.
Not an unexpected situation, as you might
imagine. Tradition required the new regime
to ask the palace staff to submit their
resignations, a perfunctory step taken as
a matter of course after each overthrow of
government. Only this time the watchman's
resignation was accepted, much to his surprise,
and at his advanced age he found himself
needing to procure gainful employment, a
difficult task for someone who spent the

previous twenty years staring into the night
looking for a lone signal flare. These are not
transferable skills, as he discovered to his
chagrin, and besides the employers of that
ancient world preferred younger workers
because they earned less and responded more
appropriately to voice commands. In various
interviews the watchman tried to describe
what it was like, staring into the darkness
night after night, trying to keep awake and
haul some meaning up from those inky depths,
keeping company with the silent yet swarming
stars, trying to pay attention and not miss
the signal although for years and lengthening
years the signal never arrived. It was all to no
avail. Once he was asked if it was really he
who first saw the light in the distance and of
course he answered that it was him and that
he was sure of it. But thinking on it later he
realized he couldn't tell. He couldn't trust his
memory, that was the pity of it all. The king
was murdered in his bath, a cathartic downfall,

and afterward someone wrote a play about it, a
spectacle followed over the years by the usual
stories, rumors and legends.

31

For hauling up buckets

When you sing the words, as opposed to just
speaking them or mere talk, it means the words
go up into the sky, if they can make it up there,
and perform at icy altitudes the great feats
of acrobatics that only words can perform.
Which might explain why the bucket haulers
union sang every week at their Friday evening
demonstrations as they marched up and down
the streets whose names we have forgotten today
for no good reason. They went on strike for the
right to not haul pails of water and other items
up and down five flights of stairs for a single fee

but instead to be paid by the bucket and by the
item which makes sense anyway if you have ever
hauled water up the steep stairs of those walk-up
flats and never spilled a drop. Never a drop
out of those buckets, never a drop out of those
pails. They also lit the lamps in the hallways and
rooms that seemed to perpetually flicker and
summon shadows forth. The strike was crushed,
of course, and no one remembers the songs they
sang because back then they had no devices with
which to record songs. Also because we want to
forget. We want to forget songs, and we want
to forget the names of streets. We know only
there were songs, and this thanks only to the
newspapers of the day containing a brief mention
or two of these events, scraps of newsprint now
barely preserved in the archives of a few minor,
outlying libraries. But if the wind over those
forgotten streets managed to grab a few snatches
of those songs and heave them across weather
fronts and political boundaries it might be
reasonable to think that today's winds preserve,

in some fashion, a few notes of those melodies
the bucket haulers sang, the notes they sang
as they marched under the banners of Friday
evening sunsets and their inconstant heavens
for what rights they thought they had, for what
rights they thought they deserved.

32

For the unexpected

The fish swam in from the ocean right up to the base of the falls. Jonah was there, standing on the rock and holding forth in his own inimitable way about voyages and leaps of faith. If a thing is worth doing it is worth doing well, he admonished the crowd, and ten thousand heads nodded, knowing what would occur next. But then the unexpected occurred, and the fish leapt straight up the falls and swallowed Jonah in one gulp, just like that. The fish with Jonah inside swam back to the ocean, and after that each spring they gathered by river to see

if the fish that swallowed Jonah would return.
For years this did not happen, the crowd left
disappointed, some even demanded their money
back, although the back of the ticket stated
clearly how no refunds would be given. Finally
one spring the fish returned and they caught it
and cut Jonah out of its stomach. He appeared
unchanged and unperturbed, and prepared to
continue his existence. After reviewing several
years of current events in old newspapers, he
embarked on a lecture tour and expected to rake
it in, but audiences were sparse, because his voice
had weakened after years in the fish's belly and
his mien turned unassertive. Eventually, he had to
get a job on the docks, looking into the holds of
ships and making lists and bills of lading, and not
being above taking bribes every now and then if
he really needed the money, if he could justify to
himself just a little bit of wickedness.

33

For being forgotten

Only a week after Jesus raised him from the dead it seemed Lazarus had been forgotten. The novelty of being brought back to life wore off completely, and not only that, but his presence among the living soon became unwanted and resented. Having considered him dead, no one was willing to once again consider him alive. These included his wife, who had already cashed in the life insurance policy and moved in with her lover, and his children who had immediately devoured half their inheritance and set their attentions on soon devouring the other half.

Oh it's you, they said to their resurrected father, not feigning anything. Even his room they repurposed for the storage - boxes and boxes of the stuff that had no other proper place in the house. So not at all light-heartedly Lazarus set out onto the open road, to see what wisdom he might wring out of its vistas and skylines. However the open road was not at all to his liking, so he joined up with a traveling circus where he became the feature in the act The Man Brought Back from the Grave. But the act flopped, largely because he had nothing much to say about being brought back from the dead. He could not describe it in a way that interested anyone. One moment he was dead, and the next moment, somehow, he was alive again. Was there some sort of bright light? There may have been, but he wasn't sure, it all happened so quickly. Listen, the circus manager said to him one day, we need to spice things up a bit. Do you see Sheila the Stripper over there, he said, pointing to a scantily costumed performer sitting

under a shade umbrella. We're going to add you
to her act. So now five times a day Lazarus sits
in a darkened corner of the stage, watching the
spotlight play with Sheila as she disrobes one
item at a time. What does this all have to do with
me, he wonders. The answer came to him, finally
and fleetingly, as buck-naked Sheila bounds
towards him and the applause swells.

34

For messages on the air

Loomis the dentist sent electronic messages
through the air. He ascended the blue ridge
mountains with kites stuffed with copper gauze
and flew them way up into the middle of the air,
yet still connected to terra firma by an insulated
wire. Earlier he invented porcelain dentures
because everyone whose teeth fell out of their
mouths deserved the chance to eat, they deserved
the chance to smile. Yet after long hours peering
into mouths he looked up into heaven, expecting
the repetition of mighty events such as the great
storm of 1859 when legislators passed their

laws outdoors at night by the light of the aurora
and the telegraph system conveyed messages of
prophetic gibberish sans batteries, sans operators,
sans everything. This inspired him. Loomis' kites
flew high into the air and spoke to one another,
while back on the rocky summits a needle on
a meter moved this way and that, proving it
had really happened and demonstrating the
importance of conversations of this sort. But
when the investors came down from New York
and Chicago the kites remained silent, although
it didn't matter because the investors were soon
to be wiped out by panics and fires. What was
there left for Loomis to do? He wrote a patent
application for his wireless telegraphy, then
erased everything and preached instead how
the world needed no alphabets and no signals.
How exhausting this all was we cannot imagine.
Towards the end of his life he judged himself
sane and invented a traveling suitcase that
doubled as a lunch counter. He could thus often
be seen having his mid-day meal on mountain

summits, gazing heavenward from whence some
sort of salvation may or may not come, then
lugging his suitcase back down the hill.

35

For chanterelle pools

Your knee will trick you all the way down. Pay no attention to it. At the end of the day you'll pull up to the chanterelle pool, nearly lame and tired and sweaty. Lovers come here for the first time, because the water is cold and clear and deeper than you think. It must be five feet deep at the base of the rock at the far end of the pool, deep enough to wade in up to your neck, deep enough to drown. After immersing yourself you sit and let the water dry on your skin, your mind pulling at invisible things in the air that can only be seen at certain hours of the day. You pull these things

together to weave a basket, to sew a shirt that
makes the wearer immortal, to build a house. You
set the house up on the bank overlooking the
stream. What a pleasant place to live, you think
to yourself. When you come back weeks later
the house is gone. In its place, you find a stone
fire ring with old ashes. You sit by the ring and
wait for a while, wondering if anyone will turn
up. You wonder if you've missed them, and fool
yourself into thinking you hadn't. So you spend
the time as it gets dark listening to the few late
summer insects compose their codas, before even
these compositions go quiet.

36

For the need for blessings

For a long time I have been a collector of
obscure blessings. Once in Ragusa I stood
outside and heard a congregation bless a certain
slant of winter light said to fall majestically
on the bare hills above the city walls on clear
afternoons, and then listened to the same
murmur bless those roofs in the town in
need of the strength to heal the holes always
appearing in them over time. If you look in
certain books you will find blessings scribbled

in the margins, although the blessing that blessed these scribblings themselves I never found, despite the painstaking search of thousands and thousands of pages. But the most obscure blessing I have looked for is the blessing of the spaces between the trees. Not one in a thousand people have heard of this, even the so-called blessing experts I am forced to call upon every now and then. Yet when you go deep into the woods themselves, there you find spaces in need of blessings and why stand in the middle of all these trees and the spaces between them and have no blessing to utter, no blessing to caress your lips? After lengthy considerations I decided the blessing must exist there in the forest itself and went looking underneath the ferns in the summer and the deep snows in the winter, listened to the black flies' impatient monologues before the streams made their midsummer quietus, and heard the thrush's exegesis on the variety of summer evenings. This is a long labor and I have only just started it, but I am committed everyday to its continuation. I pray only that I be allowed to complete it before the end of my days.

1. This is a failed translation or love letter to the first chapter of Babel's Red Cavalry, which is the model I suppose for this entire set of stories, as unapparent as that may seem. This chapter was written before the latest phase of the Russo-Ukrainian special military war. It is presented here as a kind of historical artifact.

2. Begins with the Tractate Berakhot from the Talmud concerning Hannah mother of Samuel, with a rapid segue to a legend from the 17th century Polish-Lithuanian Commonwealth. The Chagall exhibit occurred in Montreal October 1988-February 1989 and included paintings such as The Cattle Dealer.

3. The Harrisburg Express was the local name for the train running from Baltimore. Md. to Harrisburg, Pa. I believe this was a Penn Central route for many years before devolving to Amtrak.

4. A conflating of the accounts of the flood and the sacrifice of Isaac. The opening sentence comes from Bob Dylan's song Highway 61, the first verse of which refers to a killing scheduled to occur somewhere along the eponymous highway.

9. Chimney swifts are said to live almost their entire lives airborne and never touch the ground. That Brueghel's rendering of the Tower of Babel includes any depiction of swifts is not a commonly accepted interpretation.

10. Child's Ballad #12

11. A retold episode from Thoreau's expedition to Katahdin 1846. Famously Thoreau did not reach the summit of the mountain.

13. The composer Bella Bartok spent much time in the early twentieth century countrysides collecting folk songs.

14. Danilo Kis reports two accounts of Simon's

confrontation with Peter, each with distinct conclusions.

15. Based on any number of traditional songs and stories recounting the tribulations of barren women. Woody Gutherie's account of the bank robber Pretty Boy Floyd was first recorded in April 1940. The mistake in referring to the thousand dollar bill is intentional.

16. Romaine Tenney was an Ascutney, Vt. farmer. Directly in the path of the construction of interstate 91, he burned his house down in September 1964, a tragedy now nearly forgotten in Vermont and the hill country of northern New England.

18. Tradition holds that Darby Field was the first European to ascend Mount Washington in New Hampshire. The upper reaches of Mount Washington and its surrounding peaks and ridges retain snow well into the spring months.

19. For Melville's account of Pipp's spiritual

transformation, see the Moby Dick chapter The Castaway.

21. A jazz trumpeter and singer, Chet Baker was well known for his renditions of ballads such as My Funny Valentine. He fell accidentally to his death from a hotel balcony in Amsterdam.

22. David Lyle corresponded with many mid-century artists and writers. William Carlos Williams mentions and quotes him in Paterson.

24. The Wonders of the Little World, published in London in 1678 is said to be a general history of man in six books.

27. A pond with the name Unknown Pond can be found in the hills outside of Stark, NH.

28. The Split Rock lighthouse is a stone tower in Essex, NY., first constructed in 1838. The long wild ridge to its south is one of the northern-most habitats for the timber rattlesnake, and is

marked by prominent cliffs of stone plunging into the waters of Lake Champlain.

30. An imagined conclusion to the opening scene of Aeschylus' Agamemnon.

31. Few records of bucket hauling or bucket hauler unions exist.

34. Mahlon Loomis, a dentist, conducted field experiments in atmospheric electricity and wireless telegraphy during the 1860s and 1870s.

35. The chanterelle is much prized among mushroom gatherers and the spots where it grows are guarded zealously by many.

36. Ragusa is a now unused alternate official name for the city of Dubrovnik.

About the Author

Roger Lebovitz lives in Burlington, Vermont. In addition to *Obscure Blessings*, he has also written *A Guide to the Western Slope and the Outlying Areas* and *Twenty Two Instructions for Near Survival*, both published by Fomite Press.

Fomite

Writing a review on social media sites for readers will help the progress of independent publishing. To submit a review, go to the book page on any of the sites and follow the links for reviews. Books from independent presses rely on reader-to-reader communications.

For more information or to order any of our books, visit:

fomitepress.com/our-books.html

More Fomite "Odd Birds"...

William Benton
  Eye La View
Michael Breiner
  the way none of this happened
Roger Coleman
  The World Was Late
Bill Davis
  Cheap Gestures
Clare Dolan
  Museum of Everyday Life

J. C. Ellefson
   Under the Influence: Shouting Out to Walt
Stephen J. Goldberg
   Rants Raves & Ricochets
Joel Grossman
   Reading Embodied
David Ross Gunn
   Cautionary Chronicles
Andrei Guriuanu &Teknari
   Portraits of Time
   The Darkest City
Gail Holst-Warhaft
   The Fall of Athens
Sam Kerson
   Executions and Democracy
   Gaza Punishing the Innocent
Michael Jewell
   The Memoirs of a Paper Doll
Daniil Kharms
   Connections (translator Roger Lebovitz, artist
Delia Robinson)
Roger Lebovitz
   *A Guide to the Western Slopes and the Outlying
      Area*
   Obscure Blessings
   Twenty-two Instructions for Near Survival

Fomite

Pippo Lionni
  Fat Facts of Life
dug Nap
  Artsy Fartsy
  Friends
Fletcher Oakes
  Modern Mandalas
Puppeteers
  Sourdough Rising
Delia Bell Robinson
  A Shirtwaist Story
  The Waters Prevail
Claire Russell
  Dear Mr. Thoreau
Clark Russell
  Riddleville
Peter Schumann
  A Child's Deprimer
  Abrakadabra Yes No Apocalypse
  All
  All, Nothing, Nothing at All
  Bedsheet Mitigations
  *PBelligerent & Not So Belligerent Slogans from
    the Possibilitarian Arsenal*
  Bread & Sentences
  Declaration of Light/Quo Vadis

Fomite

*Diagonal Man Theory + Praxis, Volumes One
     and Two*
Erbarme dich – Have Mercy
Es is vollbracht - Mission Accomplished
Faust 3
Gaza Genocide Bedsheets
Handouts and Obligations
Kropotkin Speaks
Life and Death of Charlotte Salomon
Mister Aeschylus's The Persians
Planet Kasper, Volumes One and Two
Tears Clouds Trees
We
We Possibilitarians One and Two
Peter & Elka Schumann
     She Sits, She Rides, She Flies
Schütz, Heinrich
     Notes of Devastation
M.D. Uhser & T. Motley
     Poem A Mashup